Stalked

Ayshia Monroe

SADDLEBACK
EDUCATIONAL PUBLISHING

SADDLEBACK
EDUCATIONAL PUBLISHING
www.sdlback.com

ISBN-13: 978-1-61651-668-0
ISBN-10: 1-61651-668-2
eBook: 978-1-61247-640-7

Printed in Guangzhou, China
0612/CA21200871

16 15 14 13 12   1 2 3 4 5

Get up, Kiki! Get your butt up! Whatchu think this is, a ho-tel?"

Sherise Butler stood over her twin sister, Kiki, who was still fast asleep with the covers over her head. "Come on, Shemeka! You don't wanna to be late. Not today!"

She shook her sister through the worn white sheet. Kiki's response was to fake-snore. Sherise was not amused. Then Kiki shifted the fake-snore into a donkey's bray, and Sherise cracked up. Not that Sherise had ever seen a donkey. There weren't many donkeys in the hood where Sherise lived with her sister, their mom, LaTreece, and their long-time stepdad, Tyson Nelson.

"No donkeys in this hood. Plenty of asses though," Sherise thought with a grin.

"Why you up before the alarm?" Kiki muttered. "What time is it?"

Sherise snuck a glance at the old clock radio; the one LaTreece had bought at Goodwill for five bucks. That was what normally woke them up since they both turned in their cell phones to LaTreece and Tyson at ten thirty. LaTreece and Tyson were way stricter than anyone else's parents, grandparents, foster moms, or whatnot. Sometimes they were a damn pain. But they always took care of theirs.

"Six fifty-five," Sherise declared. "Get your butt up."

"Jeez-o! Why you trippin'? You never up before me!" Kiki pulled the covers high over her head.

Kiki had a point. Sherise was never up before Kiki, not on a school day for sure. Most school days? Sherise had to drag herself out of bed. As a rule, she hated school. She wasn't a brainiac jock like her sister. She couldn't keep up in classes or in hoops.

But Sherise had Kiki beat when it came to looks and boys. For sure.

Kiki finally sat up. She'd slept in an old Lakers shirt with Shaq's number. Sherise hooted at her sister's braids, which were tangled like a bird's nest, as Kiki rubbed sleep from her eyes.

"Just what's so funny? And what's the dealy with you all showered and dressed and made-up already?" Kiki demanded.

It was true: Sherise was ready to dip. She'd been awake since six, working her look in the apartment's single bathroom with the toilet you had to flush twice. She wanted to look good, and not just for her boyfriend, Carlos Howard. Today was a day she actually wanted to go to school: a day where she wanted to look fine for everyone.

Fortunately for Sherise, she had a lot to work with. She was petite and slender with straight hair to the middle of her back and skin like spun gold. This morning she wore a slinky black dress with a red belt and red boots. The outfit came from GG's, the clothing store at the Eastside Mall where she worked after school.

She knew she looked hot. That was good because today the whole school would have its eyes on her. She wanted every boy to want her, every girl to be jealous of her, and only Carlos to have her. She'd had the hottest dream about Carlos last night. They were in a big bed in a castle, like in the movies, and—

"What's so funny?" Kiki repeated, pulling Sherise back to reality.

Sherise pointed to the top of her sister's head.

Kiki touched her tangled braids and grimaced. "Least I don't fry it to death like some girl I know." She took in her sister. "You do look good, girl."

"Thanks. You know, I could help you with your—"

"Don't want help."

Kiki stood and stretched. She was one minute younger, five inches taller than Sherise, and all muscle-y like the girl jock she was. Actually, Sherise knew that Kiki had the right stuff to be smokin' hot if she wanted. But Kiki didn't care about being fine. She kept her hair in easy-peasy braids and always wore boring clothes and basketball kicks. Makeup was a dirty word.

LaTreece stuck her head in the girls' door. She looked a lot like Sherise, only older and thirty pounds heavier. She had on a nice dress for work, where she answered phones at the same agency where Tyson was a community development social worker. "Well, my word. Look at my Sherise!"

"It's a big day, Mama," Sherise reminded her. "They're giving out yearbooks to the whole school today. 'Member? I'm givin' a speech!"

LaTreece dead-eyed her. "You think I'd forget that?"

Tyson came up behind LaTreece. Tall and skinny with ears that stuck out more than Barack Obama's, he had short gray hair that made him seem older than his real age. Weekdays he wore what Sherise called his SWU—social work uni—dark pants, jacket, and a tie.

"You see, Sherise?" Tyson declared. "You ran for yearbook club president; you won, and now see what happens when you put your mind to something."

Tyson was a great guy, but big on teachable moments. It was a bit much at seven in the morning.

Kiki came to Sherise's rescue. "Uh, Tyson?"

"Yeah, Kiki?"

Kiki pointed at the clock radio. "Can we maybe wait on the life lessons till breakfast?"

"Yes, ma'am," he joked. "Eggs, grits, and life lessons in twenty minutes. See you in the kitchen."

LaTreece gave him a nudge. "Show them the e-mail."

"What e-mail?" Tyson smiled slyly then unfolded a sheet of paper. "Okay.

This just came in from Mr. Crandall, the guidance counselor."

"Crap," the girls said at the same time. Neither of them liked Mr. Crandall. In fact, no one liked Crandall. He'd go off on anyone at any time just to prove he had power.

Tyson shook his head. "Nah, this is good. Check it out."

He handed the e-mail to Sherise. Kiki crowded in to read it too.

Dear SCHS Parents and Guardians:

Please join the students, faculty, and staff of South Central High School in congratulating our school yearbook committee, and especially its president, Sherise Butler, on the SCHS yearbook being chosen as one of the three finalists in the High School Yearbook of the Year competition. New copies of the yearbook have been printed and will be distributed to all students at a special assembly today where Sherise and Ms. Okoro will speak. Congratulations again. Go Tigers!

Sherise grinned and bowed. "I'd like to thank all the little people who—"

LaTreece tossed the girls their cell phones. "See you at breakfast, little people."

She and Tyson went to the kitchen. Kiki headed for the shower. Sherise was alone, still holding her cell. She checked her texts. A couple had come in already today.

U the bomb, girl!

Nice. That was from Nishell Saunders, yearbook photo editor. In the last few weeks, she and Nishell had gotten a lot closer.

Way 2 go, way 2 go, way 2 go.

From Tia Ramirez, yearbook manager.
Tia had almost wrecked the yearbook by
putting in that big picture of Sherise in
Darnell Watson's arms. That picture had
made Sherise crazy. Tia had apologized,
and Sherise had forgiven her. She liked
Tia a lot, but sometimes the girl just got
too intense.

As she stood there, a new text came in.

Proud of my boo. How many
daze 2 prom?

Awww. From Carlos. She texted back
all flirty. She and Carlos hadn't done
the deed, yet. They'd talked about prom
night in three weeks as maybe being *the*
night.

U Dserv me?

She put her cell in her bag, went to the grimy bedroom window, and looked out. Their seventh floor apartment was nothing special, and neither was Northeast Towers, the project where they lived. There were two big buildings of fifteen stories each whose bricks were begging for a power washing that would never come. There was also a daycare, a meeting room where the air conditioner never worked, and a laundry room with overpriced machines whose owner must be making a flipping fortune. Outside was a crappy park with a few trees and an even crappier basketball court.

Still, it was early May, Sherise's fave time of year. School was ending in a few weeks, and she'd be working full time at GG's while her sis was getting barfed on at the Towers daycare. The trees were greening up—especially the sycamore by the basketball court that she'd loved to climb when she was a kid. The sun was warm. Everyone heading to work looked happy.

On her way to the kitchen table, she stopped at the living room computer—Tyson's agency had let him take home an old one, no way could they afford a new one—and checked out her Black-Planet page. The night before, she'd posted all about the yearbook.

More congrats. From Patrice Waters, who'd moved to Texas and was about to join the army. From Conrad Shipkins, the computer geek who had a mad crush on her in fifth grade before he moved to Detroit. And from Tarshea Williams, whose family went back to Jamaica when her dad lost his job and couldn't find another one.

Tyson had the eggs ready. As everyone ate happily, LaTreece asked

Sherise what she was planning to say in her speech. Before she could answer, the front door buzzer sounded.

Huh? A neighbor this early?

Sherise answered. It wasn't a neighbor. A flower delivery guy in a white uniform stood there with a single rose in a bud vase.

"Are you Sherise Butler?"

"Uh-huh." Sherise nodded.

"For you."

He gave Sherise the flower. She was stunned. No one had ever sent her a flower. She just stood there with the rose in her hand.

"Is there a card?" LaTreece asked. She had come over to see who was at the door. So had Tyson and Kiki.

Sherise nodded. There was a little card attached to the stem of the rose.

You the girl, S. Love you no matter what! C.

Sherise felt ready to melt. Carlos had to love her a ton to do something like this.

When it was time to leave for school, Sherise was so happy and excited she practically floated out of the apartment.

On the way to the bus stop, though, she had the oddest feeling.

She felt like she was being watched.

South Central High School was too poor to have a real auditorium like the white kids' schools uptown. The cafeteria did double duty. Sherise got there fifteen minutes before the final period assembly. When she stepped inside, practically the whole YC—yearbook club—ran over to greet her, their voices all mixed up.

"Yo, prez!"

"Sherise, you the bomb!"

"Sherise, Sherise, Sherise!"

There was Tia. She had a long braid and new glasses that actually made her look cuter. There was Nishell, with her great curvy body. Kiki, of course. And the main guys, Darnell and Jackson Beauford. Darnell was a basketball player headed to Long Beach State on a hoops scholarship. Jackson was a player, period.

About the only person who didn't run over was Marnyke Cooper. Sherise saw Marnyke hang back and smirk in her tiny red skirt and sheer top, as if to say, "I don't care how fly you think you be, Sherise. You'll never be as fine as me!"

Sherise thought Marnyke probably fell out of bed in the morning looking fly. A little taller than Sherise, with a bangin' booty and better twins, Marnyke was a guy magnet. Not only that, she hated when guys paid attention to other girls. Sherise thought Marnyke was a mean green flirt machine. Kiki liked her. Sherise never understood why.

"What you gonna say in your speech?" Nishell asked.

"I'm going to thank everyone. Even Marnyke!" Sherise cracked.

The kids laughed. They knew that Sherise and Marnyke were a long way from friends.

Sherise looked around the cafeteria. It was practically empty. The tables had been moved so that when kids filed in, they could sit on the floor. Workers were stacking yearbooks on a table at the far end of a simple wooden stage. The custodian, Ms. Apis, was setting up a mic.

"Should we show her?" Nishell asked Tia.

"Show me what?" Sherise asked.

"Watch!" Tia exclaimed.

Tia and Nishell ran over to the mini stage and tugged on two ropes against the back wall. A canvas unfurled. It was a big mural of the YC with Sherise at the center.

CONGRATS SCHS YEARBOOK CLUB AND PREZ SHERISE BUTLER!

Wow. This would be the backdrop for the assembly. Sherise was touched. The only thing that could have made this better would be if Carlos was in YC. But Carlos wasn't a joiner. Until recently, it had been a big thing for him just to come to school. *Oh well.* She'd see him at the assembly.

"Sherise?"

Sherise turned. There was Ms. Okoro, the English teacher from Nigeria who was YC advisor. Everyone called her Ms. O. Her hair was in dreads; she wore a long, colorful dress that covered her ample body and thick legs. Behind Ms. O was a fat white guy holding a heavy

TV camera and a blond white lady in a sleek black suit.

"Omigod. That's Jessica Hollander, the reporter!" Sherise gasped.

"Sherise," Ms. O said in her soft Nigerian accent, "I'd like you to meet Jessica Hollander from Eyewitness News. Jessica, this is our club president, Sherise Butler."

Jessica extended a hand. "It's good to meet you, Sherise. We're here to film the assembly. This is quite a feat for your school. I'd like to get an interview after the assembly, if you don't mind."

"That ... that ... that would be ... great!"

"Wonderful," Jessica replied. "It's just ten minutes till the assembly starts, so we want to film your speech, and—"

"Excuse me!"

Mr. Crandall stepped into the cafetorium. He had thinning hair the color of dried pigeon poop, watery blue eyes, bad taste in suits, and always looked like he'd just bitten into a lemon.

Today, he looked like he'd bitten into two lemons. He carried one of the new yearbooks.

Mr. Crandall addressed the reporter curtly. "The principal's about to make the announcement on the P.A. that the assembly's canceled. Leave."

What?

Sherise looked at Ms. O, who'd clearly had no warning, as Mr. Crandall repeated himself. "There will be no assembly today! Leave!"

Then came the booming announcement over the school loudspeakers. "Attention, students. Please remain in your sixth period classes. The assembly has been canceled. There will be early dismissal in ten minutes. Thank you."

This was no joke. There would be no assembly. But why?

When the crew was gone, Mr. Crandall assembled the shocked YC at a table. Sherise was between Tia and Nishell. She had nothing to say. Even Darnell and Jackson had nothing to say, and they always had something to say.

Mr. Crandall paced around like a strung-out crackhead. Finally he turned to the table and talked.

"I'm angry," he practically spat. "I'm disgusted. Look at this!"

He opened the yearbook to the center two pages and approached the table.

"Look!"

Omigod. Some kids gasped. Some drew in their breath. Not Sherise. She felt sick.

Long ago, Tia had joked about the first page of the yearbook being a picture of Mr. Crandall's bare butt. This actually was a picture of Mr. Crandall's bare behind. Obviously Photoshopped.

He was mugging for the camera with his hands on his own butt cheeks.

Printed across the two pages in big black letters were these words:

CRANDALL SAYS "KISS MY A**!"

Sherise moaned. This was worse than horrible. The center page was supposed to be a memorial spread about a boy who'd died in an apartment fire. Not this ... thing!

Sherise felt eyes on her. Down the table, she saw Marnyke grinning like she was having fun. In fact, Marnyke actually laughed.

Bee-yotch. But Sherise knew she couldn't worry about Marnyke right then. She was YC president. She knew she had to say something. But what?

She raised her hand. "Mr. Crandall?"

The guidance counselor nodded curtly.

"Mr. Crandall, as president of YC, I have to say that this is terrible. None of us know how this happened, and we're all sorry—"

"Put a sock in it, Sherise! Get out of here!" Mr. Crandall roared, cutting her off. "All of you, ruining our school. Go home! And when I figure out how this happened—Sherise—you will be sorrier than you have ever been in your sorry little life. Go!"

The meeting was over.

Everyone stumbled out but Sherise, Kiki, and Ms. O. Her sister and the advisor seemed to want to talk, but Sherise waved them away. She just sat there, head buried in her hands.

How could this happen? Who did this? Something had to have happened at the printer. But what? Hey! Maybe it was only in the copy that Crandall had!

Full of hope, Sherise rushed over to the stacked yearbooks. She whipped one open to the center pages, praying—

No.

There it was. Same ugly picture. Same hateful words.

Sherise opened yearbooks, one after another. All had the same photo. She felt sick all over again.

Why didn't I check out the first copy as it came off the press? Wasn't that my job?

"Sherise?"

Carlos. So handsome with his high cheekbones and close-cropped hair. He wore long gray shorts, a T-shirt, and an open sweatshirt.

"I heard what happened." He held his arms wide. She went to him. He was so tall that her head barely reached his chest.

"What am I going to do?" she sobbed. "What am I going to do?"

"You gonna figure out who did it, and then you gonna kick some butt," Carlos told her. "Everybody's gone home. Where you headed?"

Sherise shrugged and wiped her teary eyes. "Dunno. Go to work, I guess."

"I'll walk you to the bus," Carlos said.

Sherise nodded.

The walk to the bus stop this time was so different from her walk to the bus stop that morning. Then, she'd been flying. Now, she felt like hell. They passed a few kids from school who laughed and pointed.

"Nice butt shot of Crandall!" one boy yelled. Word had spread, fast.

Carlos waited with her for the bus that would take her to the mall. When it pulled up, she gave his right hand a little tug of thanks.

Then she froze. There was that weird feeling again. Like someone was watching her. She looked behind her. Nothing.

"What's wrong?" Carlos demanded.

Sherise shook her head. She was imagining things. Or maybe it was kids on the street still staring at her. Not because she was slammin', but because she'd just had her sorry ass slammed.

Yeah. That had to be it.

CHAPTER
3

It was a thirty minute bus ride from school to work. The trip took her through all kinds of neighborhoods, from the poor black one where she lived to one full of immigrants from El Salvador and then another that was all Korean. Then the bus passed a strip of auto dealers and finally stopped at the mall.

Most times Sherise loved to stare out the window and watch her city change. Today she was deep in her head.

Who did this?

What are the other kids on YC gonna think of me?

What's Mama gonna say? And Tyson?
What do I do?
How could this happen?

Sherise knew that for the first and last questions, she had to start with the printer. The yearbooks were printed by Big Boss Printing, a local company run by a former Major League Baseball pitcher whose nickname was still the Big Boss.

Sherise took out her phone. The print shop was on speed dial.

"Big Boss!" someone answered.

"This is Sherise Butler. Is Big Boss around?"

The guy at the other end laughed. "No one's around. Just me, the watchman. Such a nice day, Big Boss gave everyone the day off, 'cludin' himself. 'Cept me!" He laughed again. "Try again Monday, honey."

He clicked off, leaving Sherise hanging.

That was useless.

The bus pulled up to the mall, and Sherise got out with a bunch of shoppers. She trudged through the half-full parking lot, kicked aside a few empty foam cups that some piggy people had dropped, and entered through the west doors. GG's was two stores in, next to a formal wear shop that got stupid busy at prom time because it did rentals with just a cash deposit.

GG's sold teen and women's clothes, bags, jewelry, and low-price perfume. Rich white ladies would stick their heads in, wrinkle their Botoxed and nose-jobbed faces, and slink away. For everyone else, GG's had some great deals.

Today, the shop was empty. All Sherise wanted to do was go in, put on her name tag and work gloves, do her shift in the stockroom, and get out of—

"Sherise, you're early. What's your excuse? You cutting?"

Sherise stopped. Her boss, Juanita Gutierrez, blocked the aisle. Juanita was shorter than Sherise, with hair dyed bright red and fierce dark eyes. Today she had on a short black blouse and a mondo-tight red cotton skirt. She always wore gloves and insisted that all her employees wear gloves so they wouldn't mess up the clothes. Sherise thought this was wack. Why couldn't folks just wash their hands?

"No," Sherise managed hoarsely. "They sent us home early."

"Well, there's fifteen boxes to unpack, and ..." Juanita's voice trailed off; she looked at Sherise strangely. "You look like you've been crying, girl. What's the matter?"

"Nothing," Sherise muttered. After all, Juanita was her boss, not a friend. "Just lemme work."

Juanita didn't move. "I don't want your tears landing on my clothes. So you better talk."

"Fine."

Sherise told Juanita what had happened with the yearbook.

When she was done, Juanita whistled. "Hooboy. Who hates you?"

"What?"

"I asked, who hates you? Cause someone somewhere done messed you up, Sherise. They done messed you up bad!" Juanita's head was nodding like a Latina bobble-head doll.

"Well, this girl Marnyke doesn't like me, but she's in yearbook club too," Sherise told her.

Could Marnyke actually have something to do with it? She had laughed—

"What about that man of yours? What's his name again?" Juanita pressed.

"Carlos."

"Yeah, Carlos. The one who applied for a job here. We need to talk about that. What about him?"

Sherise was shocked that Juanita would suggest that Carlos might have ruined the yearbook. "Carlos? No way!"

"I don't mean him," Juanita explained quickly. "I mean maybe someone who hates him and got back at him by messing you up. There's people who must hate Carlos 'cause he supposedly left the life. Maybe he did something those folks don't wanna forget."

"I don't believe that." Sherise shook her head.

Juanita made a face. "It don't matter what you believe, it matters what's going down. If I was you, I'd have a talk with him. No lettuce. No onions."

Earlier in the spring, after she and Carlos had almost broken up over something stupid, Carlos had applied for a job at the store. Juanita told Sherise about it, but since that time she hadn't said a word. Now Sherise wanted to know.

"What did you decide to do 'bout Carlos anyhow?"

"What did I decide to do?" Juanita repeated. She seemed unhappy.

"That's what I asked."

"Well, if you must know," Juanita said, "there's no way he can ever work here. I did the usual check-up." She scrunched her mouth funny. "He didn't pass." Juanita waited one more moment before she added, "Come on, Sherise. Don't look at me like that. Your man is on probation."

"That's—that's—that's dumb!" Sherise stammered. "He out of the life. He don't deal. He don't run with those boys no more. Whatchu think he gonna do, steal a box of yo' panties and sell 'em on the street?"

Juanita seemed to soften. "I like how loyal you are, Sherise. I really do. But you have to see it from my place. What if there's a problem with him, and it come out that I knew he was on probation? That I knew he was once a gangbanger and hired him anyway? I'll be out of a job!"

Sherise was furious. "You don't understand the kind of life he's had."

Juanita's eyes blazed. "You think? You're the one who doesn't know anything. Look, girl. I understand the life!"

Juanita whipped off her white gloves, balled her hands into fists, and held them up for Sherise to see.

Holy, holy! Her boss had gang tattoos on her knuckles. Carlos wasn't the only one who'd been in a gang.

Juanita's tattoos were like little asterisks. Sherise wondered whether each one stood for someone she'd helped stomp.

Finally, the gloves in the store dress code made sense. Juanita didn't want to scare off her customers.

It didn't make Sherise feel any better about how Juanita was treating her man, though.

"That's even more wack, Juanita. Of everybody in the whole mall? You should understand! What is wrong wit'chu?"

"Stop," Juanita cautioned. "Stop now, Sherise."

Maybe it was because of Carlos. Maybe it was because of all that had happened with the yearbook. Whatever the reason, Sherise was too angry to stop. She kept after her boss, saying Juanita didn't have a brain and didn't have a soul.

"And most of all, Juanita? You ain't got a heart!"

Juanita's eyes narrowed; her nostrils flared. "Get out."

"What?"

"Get out. Want me to say it another way? Get out of my store before I call security and throw you out! You're fired, Sherise. You are fired!"

"Good! I'm glad I won't have to work for a twit like you!"

Sherise spun on her heels and stomped away, edging around a couple of mall janitors pushing big brooms. She headed for the west doors, seething.

Just before she reached the doors, she got that strange feeling again. Like someone was watching her. Well, whoever it was, they'd picked the wrong time. She whirled and cupped your hands.

"Whoever you are," she shouted into the mall. "Whoever you are, if you're there at all, leave me alone!"

I wish Carlos was here," Sherise muttered as she and Kiki got closer to the front door of Mio's pizza joint.

"Where he be, anyway?" Kiki asked.

"Meetin' his probation officer," Sherise said through gritted teeth. "He couldn't get out of it. He'll be here later."

She'd known about Carlos's probation meeting for a week. It was too bad. She could really use his arms around her now. She didn't know who'd be at Mio's, or what kind of greeting she might get.

It was three hours after she'd gotten fired. She'd come home on the bus in a black mood. So many things that happened today should not have happened. There shouldn't have been the mess-up with the yearbook. She shouldn't have gotten fired. And she shouldn't have that creepy feeling that some dude—if it was a dude—was scoping her out.

At dinner with Tyson, LaTreece, and her sister, she'd told them everything. Kiki had already filled in their parents about the yearbook. Sherise talked about all of it except that feeling she was being watched. She knew they'd say it was because she was stressed. Or Tyson might drop one of those crazy psychologist theories he sometimes used, how the feeling of being watched was because she was watching herself. She'd say to him that sometimes a hot dog is just a hot dog. That could make him angry.

Enough people were already angry with her for one day. Besides, Tyson was on her side.

After dinner, she and Kiki hung around for a while, and then—with Tyson and LaTreece in favor—they decided to go to Mio's Pizza Palace. Mio's was the kids' main hangout, and Sherise knew she had to show her face in public sooner or later. What else would she do? Stay home for the rest of her life?

White folks went to Starbucks, but there was no Starbucks in their hood. Instead, they had pizza joints, burger joints, chicken joints, the Ethiopian place, the Caribbean place, and a Taco Bell, all on the main drag of Twenty-Third Street near Northeast Towers. And Mio's.

Mio's was owned by a white guy named Mio. Mio's grandfather had opened the place when the area used to be white and Italian, and Mio's daddy ran it when the Italians moved out and black folks moved in. Now Mio the Third ran it. He was in his sixties, bald as a cue ball and fat as Nebraska, but he made the best pizza and sold it for a buck a slice on Friday and Saturday nights with drinks for fifty cents. At those prices, the place would be jammed even if it was run by the FBI.

Sherise, wearing the same black dress she'd worn to school, had walked over nervously with her sister.

"You ready?" Kiki asked as they neared the door.

Sherise nodded. But she still took a deep breath as they stepped inside.

"Sherise! We love you, girl!"

"Sherise! We're gonna find out who did it and jack him up!"

Sherise couldn't believe it. She had barely taken three steps into the pizza parlor when a whole bunch of her buds had come running up to greet her. There was Nishell, Tia, plus Misha and Tara, and couple of other girls from YC. There was Darnell and Jackson, and even this guy Ty, whom Tia liked.

"Did you know about this?" she asked Kiki.

Her sister smiled in response.

The only one missing was Marnyke. Even as the girls crowded around her, and the boys kind of stood back and watched, Sherise wondered once more whether all this was because of Marnyke. What did LaTreece always say? "Don't cut off your nose to spite your face?" Well, maybe Marnyke had messed up the yearbook as a way to spite Sherise even if it messed up Marnyke too.

How much would it mess up Marnyke anyway? It's not like the girl would ever use YC on a college application.

Huh. Sherise knew she had some investigating to do.

"Sit down," Nishell ordered. "We've got pizza, drinks; we'll make it a YC party."

"Ms. O stopped by. She said to tell you to be strong and hang in," Tia related. "She says she convinced Crandall it's not your fault."

"That's not all true," Jackson said.

"Well, it's mostly true," Tia retorted.

For the first time all afternoon, Sherise felt like herself. Her friends didn't hate her.

She had to say what was on her mind. "Where's Marnyke?"

No one said anything. Finally, Tia spoke up. "I asked her to come. She said she was busy."

"Busy hatin' on me," Sherise thought.

For the next hour, there was pizza, sodas, and Mio's homemade cannoli pastries. She didn't eat much because she'd just had dinner, but she did manage half a lemonade. Mostly, she tried not to think about the day. It wasn't easy. But knowing that her friends hadn't quit on her made up for a lot.

Before she knew it, she heard her name called from the front door. "Sherise!"

She looked. It was Carlos. He cut past knots of people and around orange Formica tables, and then hugged her as her friends cheered. "Glad to see you, Boo."

"How'd it go?" Sherise was careful. The YC gang didn't need to know the details of his probation meeting.

"Fine, fine," he told her.

"You hangin' with us tonight, Carlos, or you takin' our girl away?" Nishell asked.

"Up to 'your girl,'" Carlos declared.

Sherise thought for a moment. She loved her friends, but she wanted to hang with her man. If it was fine with her besties …

She turned to the YC gang. "Okay with you guys if Carlos and I dip?"

"So good with me and Darnell," Jackson quipped. "A whole buncha girls and three guys, I like my odds."

"You're a pig, Jackson," Tia accused.

"Maybe," Jackson agreed. "But I'm a pig you wish you could poke!"

Everyone laughed at Jackson's dirty joke. Carlos and Sherise said bye to everyone. Sherise gave Nishell some money for her tab, and then they headed west on Twenty-Third Street. There was this place they'd been hanging lately, near the river that cut through the city. There were benches and a paved strip for people to walk on and fish from, though the river was so dirty that Sherise couldn't imagine touching a fish from that water, let alone eating it.

Even at night the place by the river was safe. Best of all, it was free.

As they walked, Sherise told Carlos how she'd gotten fired and what Juanita had said that maybe an enemy of Carlos's had messed up the yearbook.

Carlos's answer shocked her a little.

"It's possible," he told her as they got to their favorite bench and shooed away some sparrows. "I don't think so, but it's possible."

"Who? Who would do that?"

"Dunno," Carlos muttered. "This cholo named Chaco told me he'd hurt me real bad some day. Dunno where he is. I could ask around."

Sherise didn't know whether Carlos should do that or not. On the one hand, it would be good to know. On the other hand, it would put him back in touch with people that she didn't want him to be talking with at all. Ever.

"You do what you think is right," she said quietly.

She cared so much for him. He'd sent a rose to her that morning. She hadn't even thanked him for that yet. What was wrong with her?

She was about to tell him how much that rose meant to her when she got a better idea. She wouldn't say a word. She'd just do something for him that she hoped would mean as much.

And it don't have to do with s-e-x, either.

Carlos checked his cell. "It's time," he said.

"Time for what?"

He pointed to the east where a bunch of buildings punched up into the night sky. "I've got this all scoped out."

Sherise was clueless. "What scoped out?"

Carlos put his hands over her eyes. "Just wait."

She rested her head on his broad chest as Carlos kept his hands on her eyes for what seemed like five minutes.

Finally, he pulled them away and pointed to the eastern sky. "Look!" he ordered.

Sherise looked. What she saw was a full moon, now higher than the highest building. But it was no regular white full moon. This one was ruddy red, almost maroon.

"Total eclipse," Carlos explained. "I'm glad you wanted to come out here."

"An e-what?" Sherise could barely take her eyes off the gorgeous moon.

"Eclipse of the moon. Moon goes around the earth, shadow of the earth gets between the earth and the sun, a little light bends around, and that's what you got," Carlos told her with a smile. "Doesn't happen much. In fact, this is the first one I've ever seen in person. I'm glad it's with you."

She eyed him curiously. "Carlos Howard, how you know about this stuff?"

Carlos smiled a little shyly. "Don't tell no one, but since I saw Will Smith in *Independence Day*, I wanted to be an astronaut."

Sherise had no idea. She was dazzled. "Well, that's what you should be, then."

Carlos laughed in a way that wasn't funny. "Yeah, right. First ex-gangbanger astronaut. First one with a rap sheet. First one who'll be lucky to get through high school. Astronaut? Ain't gonna happen."

"Don't never say never," Sherise told him.

She kissed him. He kissed her back. It got very hot, very fast. In fact, the only thing that cooled it off was the arrival of a bunch of people with a telescope to watch the eclipse.

Sherise took a look through the telescope. The moon was huge and stunning. But she still would have rather had the people never show up.

Carlos walked her back to Northeast Towers. There was another hot kiss near the door to her building. Then he left her to catch the last bus back to his own hood where he lived with his mother. Sherise knew all about his mother. His mother was no LaTreece. He couldn't even leave money in his room because his mother would steal it to buy drugs.

After he left her, she followed him to the street just so she could watch his long, sexy strides. She watched him all the way to the bus stop.

"You in deep, girl," she told herself as she started back to her building. "You in so deep wit' this boy."

She was in deep. She liked it. Even after the day she'd had, the idea that her man was Carlos Howard made everything better.

She was halfway to the building when she got that weird feeling again.

Someone was definitely watching her. Had Carlos come back?

She whirled around and peered into the darkness. "Carlos? That you?"

Nothing. But she could feel eyes on her.

This time, it scared her. It scared her as much as she'd ever been scared in her life.

CHAPTER

5

It was awful. There was definitely someone watching her. And now he was coming!

No time to make it to the building. Sherise started running. Her heart pounded so hard she could hear the beats and feel hot blood in her veins. Sweat poured from her brow before she'd gone thirty feet.

She could hear feet smacking the sidewalk behind her as she ran out of the complex and turned onto Twenty-Third. She bolted, dodging people, hearing the feet behind her—heavy, male, scary—come closer.

"Someone's chasing me!" she screamed.

No one did anything. In fact, folks laughed.

"Why you runnin', Sherise? You gotta pee or something?" Marnyke was there, taunting her. "Maybe you gotta poo! Don't poo in yo' panties, Sherise!"

Sherise found herself at the front door of Mio's. She slammed the door shut, but Mio didn't turn around. She could see her stalker through the glass door: tall, beefy, with his face blacked out by a mask.

No! He punched out the door, smashing it to lethal confetti.

Sherise screamed again. "Somebody, please, help me! What? What the—?"

She found herself being shaken awake by her sister.

"Wake up, Sherise! Wake up! You havin' a nightmare!"

Sherise sat up. Her body was wet with cold sweat. Her heart pounded. She could still feel hot blood in her veins. But she was in her bed, in her room, safe. She looked at the clock radio: 5:51 a.m.

Yes. It had been a dream. A frightening, terrible dream that felt real.

The night before, when she'd had that creepy sense of being watched, she'd come right inside. The security guy was on duty in the lobby, thank God. She'd taken the elevator upstairs and let herself into the apartment. Teeth brushed, face washed, she was in bed and asleep before Kiki even came home from Mio's.

What a terrible dream.

"What was you dreamin'?" Kiki asked. Her voice was full of concern.

Sherise shook her head. "Don't want to talk about it."

———

"Well, sister, you done woke me at five fifty in the morning, so you'd better talk about it," Kiki insisted gently. She was sitting on Sherise's bed, wearing a bra-top and basketball shorts. "I'm not going back to sleep till you do."

Sherise knew Kiki was fierce when she put her mind to it, and Kiki was puttin' her mind to it now. Plus, Sherise needed to get it out. Who better to tell than her sister?

She shared the story of last night with Carlos. The eclipse, the kisses, the walk home, everything. And then ...

"Someone's watchin' me, Kiki. I swear."

Kiki frowned. "You seen somebody?"

"Nope. But that don't mean it ain't happening."

Kiki frowned again. "I guess that's true. What do you think we should do?"

Sherise had a bad thought. What if that guy Chaco, who Carlos knew from his old life, had been the one to get the yearbook messed up? Maybe Chaco wasn't done. Maybe Chaco was out to get her.

She swallowed hard. That wasn't crazy.

"I'm not sure," Sherise muttered.

"I think you gotta tell Mama and Tyson," Kiki decided. "They'll know what to do."

"Yeah," Sherise agreed.

"And I'll be right there with you," Kiki promised.

That's exactly what they did, at the kitchen table, when her mom and Tyson got up. The adults looked at each other when she was done.

"You know what I'm thinking, Tyson?" LaTreece asked.

Tyson nodded. "Sure do. Let's get dressed. We're going to the police."

Even at nine on a Saturday morning, the Northeast Precinct Police Station was a zoo. There'd been a drive-by the night before near school, plus a party had gotten out of hand because a bunch of home-boys had thrown bottles from a rooftop on people below. The precinct was so full there was hardly any place to sit.

Sherise got the drill fast. If you had a complaint, you had a minute to tell it to the desk sergeant who decided if your problem was urgent. If your problem wasn't urgent, you waited.

The desk sergeant—an old guy prob-ably a year from retiring—did not think Sherise had an urgent problem. Sherise and her family had to wait. And wait. It took almost two hours before they got to meet with a lady cop named Chan who was so small and thin that Sherise wondered how her gun and nightstick didn't tip her over.

Chan had a desk in the middle of a room with a lot of other desks. There were only two chairs. Chan took one. Sherise took the other. Her family stood behind her.

Tyson spoke first. "Officer, my stepdaughter thinks someone is spying on her. Following her. And maybe that some gang guy is out to get her."

Officer Chan rubbed her eyes wearily. "How about if your stepdaughter— Sherise, right?—tells me herself."

Sherise did. Chan took a few notes. "Anything going on in your life that I should know about, Sherise?"

"What do you mean?" Sherise asked.

"Anything that might make you upset? Boyfriend problems?"

"I don't have boyfriend problems!" Sherise exclaimed.

Chan turned to Tyson. "You're Tyson Nelson, right? The social worker?"

Tyson nodded. "That's right. Have we met before?"

Chan shook her head. "No. I'm new. But my boss says you're in here all the time, wanting us to help someone or another. A lot of times it turns out to be nothing."

Sherise saw Tyson's nostrils flare, which only happened when got upset. Yet her stepdad kept his voice calm.

"Officer Chan, I'm a community development social worker. My job is to help people who come to me. Sometimes these people need help from the police. Sometimes it turns out to be nothing. But isn't it better to be safe than sorry?"

The cop's eyes narrowed. "Of course. But we're very busy here, Mr. Nelson, as you may have seen. Fighting *real* crime. We don't have the time to deal with little girl bull— well, feelings."

Huh. Sherise knew what she was about to say. She might be wrong about what was goin' down. But she was not some little girl!

LaTreece put a hand on Sherise's shoulder. "Honey, I think we'd better go."

Sherise looked right at Chan. "You better hope I'm wrong," she told the Asian cop. "Because if I'm right and you guys don't help me, there's gonna be hell to pay. And I'm gonna make you pay it!"

On the walk back to Northeast Towers, Sherise did a lot of thinking. She didn't like Chan's attitude. But maybe the cop had a point. She had been under a lot of stress. Maybe all this was in her mind.

Ain't nothin' weird goin' on now, is there?

By the time the elevator doors opened on the seventh floor, Sherise was doing even better. She hadn't felt watched all the way home. About the yearbook, there was still stuff she could do. She could—

"My word. Who are those from?" LaTreece exclaimed and pointed to the door.

On the doormat was a huge bouquet of roses. A dozen. No, two dozen.

Sherise rushed over to see if there was a card. Yes. There was a card. A beautiful one. For her.

S—I am the man for you. C.

CHAPTER
6

Would you like a card to go with that?"

The clerk at the flower store smiled warmly. She was an older woman with one of the biggest Afros that Sherise had ever seen. She wore a long flowing dress, like something Ms. O might wear, and a dozen silver bracelets on her left wrist.

Sherise nodded and smoothed out a small wrinkle in her gray blouse. She'd never ordered flowers for anyone before. "Can I write it myself?"

"That would be lovely," the woman said. "Are they for your mother?"

"Boyfriend," Sherise confided.

The woman leaned in and winked. "You sure you don't want to buy him the new *Call of Duty*?"

"No. I'm not sure. But I'm sending him these anyway."

The woman laughed. "Here's a pen and a nice card. Card's on the house. Do your thing, girl."

The woman moved off to help another customer. Sherise wondered what to write. She stared at the blank card and then picked up the pen.

Dear Carlos,

I'm sorry I'm not good at words like my sister, but what I write is from my heart. When I got the one rose from you on Fri morning, I couldn't believe it. It made my heart sing. Then I came home just a bit ago to find a whole bunch more roses with your B-U-T-ful note! I have a dream for you. I want to be with you when you go to the stars.

xoxox,
Sherise

It was Sunday—Sherise had spent Saturday night hanging at home. Every so often she tried Marnyke's cell. Marnyke didn't pick up or answer her texts. What was up with that? Kiki and Marnyke were friends, so Sherise had Kiki try Marnyke too. Nothing. It got her suspicious of Marnyke all over again.

After she and her family went to church, Sherise had made a detour to this flower shop.

She sealed the envelope and gave it to the lady. She'd already paid for the mixed bouquet and special Sunday delivery. It cost a lot. Fifty bucks was a lot of money, and she didn't have a job anymore. But Carlos was worth it.

"Where to?" the clerk asked.

"Excuse me?"

"I need to know the address for the driver."

The address? Sherise had only ever been to Carlos's place once, and that was to drop him off. She knew the neighborhood—he lived in a hood even worse than hers—but not the exact address.

"I'm not sure," she told the clerk. "Let me find out."

How could she do that without telling him what it was about? Oh! She knew!

She quickly sent a text. He texted back. Texts were flying back and forth in no time.

U Home, Boo?

Uh Huh. How come?

Surprize

Luv surprizes. You the prize?

4 Me 2 Know, U to Find Out

When I gonna find out?

Addy?

422 Bancroft

Good job. Stay home

U comin?

Just B home

Yes, ma'am

There it was. The address. He'd be home. Of course, he was expecting that Sherise would be the "surprize," as she put it. That surprise was coming, but not today.

What did Ms. O always say? That Nigerian proverb about patience? "It is little by little that a bird builds its nest."

She gave his address to the nice lady. "Here's where."

The woman nodded. "I'll text you when he gets them. He's a lucky young man."

Sherise grinned, big time. She thought she was as lucky as he was.

Now she could use a little luck with something else. As she left the flower shop, she punched in a number she'd dug up online.

"Hullo?" a hoarse voice answered.

"'Bout time you answered your home phone. This is Sherise Butler," Sherise said. "I want answers, and I want them now."

Sherise saw Nishell in front of Big Boss Printing. Her friend wore jeans, a white men's shirt, and flip flops. Though Nishell was probably a size 16, she rocked the jeans. As usual, her camera was around her neck. About the only time she didn't have it with her was in school.

With her was Jackson Beauford, Mr. Flirt-with-anyone-who-breathes. He wore a plaid short-sleeve shirt and shorts so low that they seemed to hit his ankles. Sherise hated that look, but Nishell didn't seem to mind. Nishell and Jackson had been on-again, off-again for most of the year.

Guess today be on-again.

"How'd you get Big Boss to open up on a Sunday?" Jackson asked.

"Told him I'd call that TV lady if he didn't," Sherise explained. "I asked Tia to come, but she's working at the bakery."

Just then the front door opened. Big Boss motioned for them to come in. He wore a suit and tie; Sherise figured he must not have changed after church, either. He knew Sherise and Nishell; Sherise introduced Jackson.

"Call me Big Boss," the owner said. "Everyone else does."

He motioned the kids over to his desk at the front of the shop. There were a few flat screen monitors on it.

"Did you figure out what happened?" Sherise asked bluntly.

"I've been doin' some investigating," Big Boss told them. He clicked a mouse. One of the monitors lit up with the centerfold page of the yearbook: the correct page with the memorial for the boy who'd died in the fire.

"We're all computerized," Big Boss explained. "Pages get set on this computer network, and then they're sent to a separate printer server. That server controls the presses and everything that happens after that."

Sherise was impatient. "We know all that. We want to know what happened."

"Look for yourself," Big Boss said defensively. He clicked again. "Here's the upload to the printer server. It has the yearbook attached. The right yearbook. With the right pages."

He enlarged the screen. There it was. His upload order with the right attachment.

"Yup," Jackson commented. "That's the right one, all right."

Nishell was the one who figured it out first. "What are you sayin', Big Boss? That it got changed after you sent it to the server?"

Big Boss nodded. "That's exactly what I'm sayin'. The order went in at the end of the day on a Tuesday. Printing started in the morning on Wednesday. I didn't even look at the yearbook till Ms. Okoro called and said there was a problem."

Jackson hooted. "Day-um! Big Boss, you got hacked!"

Sherise was numb. *Hacked? How could that have happened?*

"Did one of your workers do this?" Sherise pressed.

Big Boss shook his head angrily. "Can't be. I'm the only one with the password. I don't share it. And don't you be lookin' at me like that, kids. It wasn't me!"

Sherise nodded. Big Boss had a point. Still, someone had hacked into his printer server.

The question was, who?

"I could bring in a tech guy to try to figure it all out," Big Boss mused. "But the damage is done. I told your advisor that I'd just reprint—"

Sherise exploded again. "It's too late for that!"

Just then she got that weird feeling. They were sitting right in the line of sight of the front glass door. Was someone watching her again?

She glanced over at the door. No one there. But was that a shadow on the floor? *Yes!*

She jumped up and ran the few feet to the door, hollering, "Show yourself! Stop watching me! Stop it! Stop it!"

She flung open the door and looked both ways. Nothing but Sunday traffic on Twenty-Third Street: street vendors, shoppers, and folks out walking on a gorgeous Sunday. Nothing wrong. Nothing strange.

—

Jackson and Nishell ran out to her.

"What just happened?" Nishell demanded.

Sherise shook her head. She was so frustrated. "I don't know."

Big Boss came outside too. "You okay, Sherise?"

She nodded. Maybe she really was just stressed.

"I'll call in the tech guy," Big Boss told her.

"How long will it take to figure it out?" Sherise asked.

Big Boss gazed right at her. "I have no idea. Truth is, if the hacker knew what he was doing, we may never know."

Sherise took a few steps and leaned against the front window of the print shop. Her knees felt like rubber as Big Boss's words echoed in her head.

"We may never know."

That wouldn't work. She had to know. She was in charge of YC. It was her job to know what happened and her job to fix it, if it could be fixed.

She was about to tell Big Boss to get ten tech guys if he needed to when her cell chimed with an incoming text. Distracted, she took out her cell and read it.

Flowers delivered!—The Flower Place

Honestly, it was hard for her to get excited over the flower delivery after what she'd just heard from Big Boss. Then her cell sounded again. Another text. This one was from Carlos. It made her feel faint to read.

Not good faint, either. Bad faint.

WE NEED TO TALK. NOW!

Sherise was happy when Nishell said she would walk to Baldwin Park with her—that's where Sherise and Carlos decided to meet since it was halfway between her hood and his. Sherise was glad for the company. She wanted to talk about Marnyke with Nishell. The more she thought about it, the more she thought Marnyke was involved with the yearbook thing. After all, hadn't Marnyke practically laughed with glee when Crandall had pitched his fit? How wrong was that?

"I keep thinking Marnyke might have done it," Sherise said as they neared the park.

"You sayin' Marnyke is the one who broke into Big Boss's server?" Nishell asked doubtfully. "I wish it were true. That would make it easy. But the girl got an I.Q. somewhere between one and two."

Sherise shook her head. "You don't have to be smart to get what you want. All you gotta be is willing to do what a boy wants. Least when you look like Marnyke look and dress like she dresses, you feel me?"

They waited for a light to change so they could cross the street. Even when it turned green, Nishell didn't move.

"Lemme make sure I get you," Nishell responded. "You actually think Marnyke got a boy to hack into Big Boss's server and change the photograph."

Sherise edged to her left so a young white mother pushing a fancy baby carriage could pass. Baldwin Park was in a white neighborhood that cut between the Towers and Carlos's hood. It was one of the nicest parks in the city. It was also filled with cops.

"Well, why not? She didn't do jack in the yearbook," Sherise went on. "That was all you, me, and Tia. Think how she treated you when you was tight with Jackson the first time, because she thought if she couldn't have Jackson, no one should. She hates that Carlos and me is going out, because she can't have him."

Sherise was on a roll. "She laughed when all this went down on Friday. Laughed! Like she was glad it happened. The whole YC was at Mio's on Friday night, and she can't even answer her texts! I mean it, Nishell. I think she did it, and now she won't face us."

They started across the street. Nishell scratched at a red spot on her right arm. "I don't know, Sherise. I don't love Marnyke any more than you do. But—"

"But nothing." Sherise had made up her mind. "She can run from me, but she sure as shoot can't hide."

"Fine with me. Good luck. Hey, there's Carlos." Nishell pointed to an asphalt path that led to the park duck pond.

Carlos spotted Sherise. He trotted over and embraced her as Nishell stood by. He wore baggy jeans and a white undershirt. Sherise caught Nishell looking as Carlos had her wrapped in his strong arms.

She wished Jackson would hug her like this, Sherise realized. She wished it too. *Nishell still don't trust her man. Not a hundred percent.*

Sherise and Nishell filled Carlos in on what had happened at the printer. "It was hacked, huh?" he asked.

Sherise nodded. "Seems that way."

"Sounds like an inside job. We know anyone who works for Big Boss?" Carlos asked.

Sherise and Nishell exchanged a helpless glance. What an obvious question! But they hadn't asked. Well, now they would the next time they talked to Big Boss.

"You good from here?" Nishell asked Sherise.

"I'm good."

Sherise hugged her friend. Nishell was a sturdy girl. Maybe that's what happened if you used to live in a homeless shelter like Nishell did. You either got beat up by it, or you beat it. Nishell beat it.

"I'll text you," Sherise told her friend.

Nishell took off. Carlos and Sherise walked together toward the park's large duck pond. Sherise couldn't help but notice that they were the only non-white people in the whole park.

"You said you had to talk to me," she prompted Carlos. "What's up?"

Carlos put his arm around her. "Two things. One good, one not so good."

"Good news first," Sherise urged.

"Okay," Carlos said as they got close to the pond. Someone had left a pile of stale bread by the water. Carlos tossed in some of the scraps. Ducks quacked and swam for them at top speed. "You know that guy Chaco? The one I was afraid might have been trying to hurt you?"

"Yeah?"

Carlos flipped more dry bread at the hungry mallards. "It can't be him. He's doing time in Texas. Three to five."

"That's good, right?" Sherise was relieved. That it wasn't Chaco made it a little more likely it was Marnyke. "What's bad?"

Carlos took her by the hands. He seemed to have a hard time meeting her eyes. "I don't know how to say this, Boo, so I'll just say it. Those flowers you sent me? They're dope. I just—I just wish I'd sent the ones that you got."

"What?" Sherise exclaimed so loudly that the ducks in the water moved away.

"I didn't ... I never ... sent you ... any flowers." Carlos had trouble getting the words out. "I didn't send flowers."

Sherise felt sick to her stomach all over again. "Carlos. If you didn't send them ... who did?"

"Umm ... Juanita?" Carlos tried a joke.

"I'm serious." Sherise was already starting to wonder if it was the person she thought, but couldn't prove, was watching her.

"I don't know," Carlos admitted.

"It's just that I've still got that scary feeling sometimes, like someone's watching me. It happened in Big Boss's office," Sherise said. She hadn't told Carlos about her feeling yet. She hadn't wanted to worry him. But she was worried now. She threw the last of the dry bread into the water.

"That's because someone is. Look."

Carlos indicated with his chin the police patrol car fifty feet away. There were two cops inside, eyes right on them.

"FDWB, that's our crime," Sherise cracked.

Carlos didn't get it until Sherise explained. "Feeding Ducks While Black."

Carlos laughed and embraced her. It seemed that he was about to kiss her when her cell sounded with an incoming call. She checked caller ID.

Unavailable.

"Hello?" she answered, thinking maybe it was Big Boss.

She heard someone at the other end breathing.

"Hello?"

Nothing.

"Hello?"

Nothing.

"Go away!" she shouted into the phone and clicked off.

Before she could even tell Carlos what had just happened, her cell sounded again, this time with an incoming text. There was no return number.

> S—I hope you loved the flowers!
> Both times!

She started sweating. Breathing hard. Shaking just a little. The truth could not be ignored. She was being stalked, and it was getting worse. Who was watching her? Why? And most of all, how much danger was she in?

Sherise pressed her nose against the fence that surrounded the rooftop of her building at Northeast Towers and gazed at the sunset. It was the oddest thing. She knew she was being stalked. That was bad. But she knew her feelings and suspicions hadn't been crazy. That was good. And now everyone believed her because her cell phone didn't lie.

Carlos was up there with her. Tyson had invited him for dinner after the frightening phone calls in the park. It was the first time that Carlos had shared a meal with her whole family.

Carlos was so smart. Sherise thought back to what happened that day. He made them wait by the police car until Kiki and LaTreece drove over to pick them up. It was a good thing too. That sick dude called Sherise back like five times. Unavailable, her behind!

Here at home, Sherise felt safe again. Tyson and LaTreece—both in shorts and short-sleeve shirts—were barbecuing pork ribs. Kiki was setting the picnic table while Carlos and Sherise stood together by the fence, watching the city drop into the night.

"You see that bright star in the sky? Above where the sun's going down?" Carlos asked.

"Uh-huh."

"That's no star. That's a planet. That's Venus."

"Really?" Sherise asked, mock-wide-eyed.

"Really." Carlos seemed ready to give a speech on the difference between stars and planets when Sherise poked him in the ribs.

"I know the diff between a star and a planet, Starman," she told him. "Planets go 'round the sun. Stars are what you see when you kiss me."

"For sure," Carlos agreed.

"Kids? Let's eat!" Tyson called.

They gathered at the table. Sherise sat between her sister and Carlos with Tyson and LaTreece across from them. Tyson put his hands out to say grace. He only did this at special meals.

It must be special because Carlos is here.

Everyone held hands.

"Lord, thank you for our food and for these fine young people at our table with us, in Jesus' name, Amen." Tyson declared.

—

"Dig in, everyone," LaTreece instructed. She put three ribs on Carlos's plate before he could even blink. "Hope you're hungry, Carlos."

"Yes, ma'am," Carlos said politely.

"Don't call her ma'am, and don't call me sir," Tyson told him as LaTreece passed around the ribs, potato salad, and sliced tomatoes. "No need to sound like a dentist."

"Yes, sir," Carlos responded. Everyone laughed.

"I wanted to say that you did exactly the right thing with Sherise today," LaTreece remarked to him. "That was very respons—"

Sherise's cell sounded again. Her blood ran cold when she saw who was calling.

Unavailable.

"It's him again," she moaned.

"Don't answer," Kiki commanded.

It wasn't like she had a choice. Before it could sound again, LaTreece snatched up the phone and barked into it, "You stay away from my daughter!"

LaTreece clicked off, and Sherise saw Carlos gazing at her mom with respect. Sherise realized that Carlos's mom had probably never stuck up for him like that in his life. She knew that half the time, Carlos didn't know where his mom was sleeping. Or with who.

Right then, Sherise felt a lot of thanks for her own mom.

"I guess we need to figure out what to do," Tyson said.

"How about if we eat first?" Kiki suggested. "I've been playin' hoops all afternoon, and I'm starvin'."

For the next few minutes, there was nothing but chewing and drinking. The ribs were good. Really good. On any other night, Sherise would have eaten four of them. But not tonight. Not after those phone calls.

There was dessert planned—berries and ice cream—but LaTreece decided to wait to serve it till after they talked.

"I think we should go back to the police," Tyson suggested.

Kiki scoffed, "That didn't work the first time."

"There's new evidence," their stepdad pointed out.

Sherise shook her head. "They'll say it's a prank. They'll ask if somebody don't like me. I'll say Marnyke—don't look at me that way, Kiki, she don't like me, get over it—and then they'll say get out of the station."

"Marnyke's got nothing to do with this," Kiki told her sister.

"Then it would be nice if she'd answer a damn text," Sherise told her. She turned to her mom and stepfather. "I have another idea. We try to catch this guy on our own."

Her mom protested. "How do you plan to do that? I won't let you put yourself in danger!"

"And I won't let that happen," Carlos promised. "No matter what. I'm not lettin' Sherise out of my sight."

Tyson stood and paced. As the evening turned to night, safety lights came on and bathed the rooftop in white light. Sherise thought it made things spooky.

"Carlos has a point," Tyson said. "No matter what we do, Sherise, I want someone with you all the time. Carlos here, your sister, kids at school, whatever. When I say all the time, I mean all the time. No exceptions."

Sherise pointed at Tyson as her idea got clearer in her mind. "But that's just what I mean. If I'm watched all the time, then maybe it's safe for me to get this person to show himself."

"How you plan to do that?" Kiki wondered.

"By using myself as bait."

There. She'd said it.

Sherise saw her folks look at each other and have a whole talk with their eyes, like couples sometimes do.

"Okay," LaTreece finally said. "You ain't a little kid anymore. It's not like the police are lined up to help you. What do you have in mind?"

Sherise had thought it through. "If he calls me again, I talk to him. Tell him I'll meet him tomorrow after school under the big tree by the basketball court."

"I'll be watching you all the way," Carlos assured her.

"I'll bring the whole YC," Kiki agreed.

"And I'll have ten men from the community association," Tyson chimed in. "I'll grab the guy and march him to the po-lice myself!"

That's what Sherise wanted more than anything in the world. Even more than an answer to what had happened with the yearbook. The yearbook was just paper and hurt feelings. This was life and death, maybe. She wanted to turn this guy over to the cops and show them that they needed to spend more time protecting people and less time making folks feel like they might be crazy. Then they could figure out who he was and why he was doing what he was doing.

Sherise thought that if he was working with Marnyke, and he saw all those people watching her, he probably wouldn't even show up.

Just after LaTreece and Tyson took some of the dishes downstairs, Kiki got a text. She looked at it and then at her sister.

"It's Marnyke," she reported.

"What'd she say?" Sherise demanded.

"Nothin' much. Just 'Hi.' "

"Ask her why she's been hiding from me. Ask her why she being such a bee-yotch!" Sherise demanded.

Kiki shook her head. "You got somethin' to say to my friend, Sherise? You say it."

"Fine," Sherise told Kiki through gritted teeth. She took out her own cell and pressed in Marnyke's number. "I will. I hope she's ready."

The call went straight to voice mail.

Sherise growled angrily. "She be pissing me off all over again!"

There was no doubt about it. Marnyke was still dodging her.

"Maybe it's about the yearbook," Sherise thought. "Maybe it's about the stalker. And maybe, just maybe, it's about both."

CHAPTER

9

Monday morning. Just like the previous Friday, Sherise was up before Kiki. This day, though, it wasn't because she was excited to go to school. In fact, she was scared to death.

She was scared about what might happen if and when she talked to Marnyke. She was scared about what might happen with Mr. Crandall. She was scared what would happen when the stalker called her. She was scared what would happen if the stalker didn't call her. He hadn't called back at all after LaTreece had told him off. In order to set the trap, she had to talk to him. She just had to.

She dressed simply: black sandals, black matador cotton pants, and a red V-neck blouse with lace across the V. While Kiki still slept, Sherise went to the family computer. No matter what else happened today, there was an e-mail she needed to send. She wrote carefully and spell checked it twice. She didn't want any goofs.

Dear Juanita,

I guess you never expected to hear from me. I am writing to say that I am sorry for how I acted with you in the store on Friday. I was upset, and I have a lot of reasons to be upset. I did not have any reason to get that upset with you even if I was mad at you. There are better ways to be mad at someone than to yell at them. I do not expect you to give me my job back, but I hope you will forgive me.

    Yours truly,

    Sherise Butler

She read it over. As she did, Sherise realized that no matter how mad she got at Marnyke when she talked to her—whenever that would be—she shouldn't yell at her any more than she should have yelled at Juanita.

"Whatchu doing on the computer?" Kiki asked. She'd come out so quietly Sherise hadn't heard her.

"Sending an 'I'm sorry' e-mail to Juanita in case I die today," Sherise answered.

"You're not gonna die. It's gonna be okay."

Sherise shrugged. "Hope so." She pressed Send. The e-mail was on its way to Juanita at the store website.

"Sherise, there's gonna be like a dozen people watching your little butt from the moment you leave the building till the moment you come—"

Sherise's cell sounded.

Unavailable.

"It's him," Sherise breathed.

"You don't have to answer if—"

Yes, she did. Now was no time to turn into a wuss.

She picked up. "Hi, this is Sherise!"

"Uh ... Sherise? Good morning! Is that really you?"

Wow. The guy sounds young. Maybe he's faking his voice.

"Yeah, it's me, who this be?" Sherise tried to stay upbeat.

"My name doesn't matter. Not yet," the guy said.

For sure he's our age. Someone Marnyke knows?

"Well, I'm assed out with all the hard-to-get," Sherise told him, her voice friendly. "What say we meet? I ain't gonna give you a chin check."

There was quiet. Then …

"Really? You want to meet me?"

"Word. I'd love to know who this boy is, payin' me all this mind, sendin' me flowers, and whatnot. How about this afternoon under the big tree by the b-ball courts at Northeast Towers? How about four thirty?"

"That'd be great! It's a date!" The guy sounded so excited.

"Okay," Sherise said. Then she loaded the trap with extra bait. "I'd tell you I was gonna be wearing black and red, but I think you already know what I look like."

"Kinda. I've kinda been watching you."

"I kinda noticed," Sherise told him. "It's kinda excitin'. So, four thirty. See you there. Do me a favor?"

"What's that?" the guy asked.

"Please don't call me at school today. I got a big day."

"Sure, Sherise. Anything for my girl."

Anything for my girl? How disgusting was that?!

"Well, later." Sherise clicked off and made a face at her sister. "That sucked."

"You did great," Kiki marveled. "You were so cool. Lemme use the bathroom quick, and then I'll walk you to school. Tia and Nishell are meetin' us downstairs. Girl, you got an entourage."

"But not your bestie, Marnyke," Sherise noted sourly.

Kiki frowned. "No. I don't think so. Be right back."

Kiki headed for the bathroom, leaving Sherise alone. Well, she'd get her shot at

Marnyke eventually unless the girl who thought she was God's gift to the male half of the planet moved to Venus. Even so, she could be patient. Marnyke would come back.

Very few cute boyz on Venus.

It turned out that she didn't have to wait long.

When she and Kiki stepped out into the warm May sunshine, Marnyke was there. She wore a gray skirt, dark boots that had to be hot in this weather, and a black pushup bra under an orange shirt with beaded sleeves. Sherise saw bags under her eyes that Marnyke had tried and failed to hide with makeup. She looked tired.

"Can we talk, Sherise?" Marnyke asked softly. "Tia and Nishell be waitin' at the street for you. Kiki? Give us some space."

Sherise stared her down. "I'd love to talk to you. Whatchu think I've been trying to do all weekend?" She turned to her sister. "Go wit' Nishell and Tia. Tell 'em I got business to take care of. Let them walk in front of us. You walk behind."

Kiki nodded. Sherise and Marnyke started toward Twenty-Third Street. It was a twenty minute stroll from Northeast Towers to SCHS. No need for the bus today. She needed time to talk to Marnyke. Sherise wasn't going to yell at her. But she wasn't going to be kind either.

"Why you been such a bee-yotch, Mar?"

"Whatchu mean?"

Sherise felt anger well up in her throat. It felt good. She was angry at what happened to the yearbook. She was angry at her stalker. But she didn't really know who to blame there. Here it was so clear. Marnyke had treated her so badly.

"You know 'zactly what I mean. When the yearbook thing happened, you laughed. When everyone came to Mio's that night, you wasn't there. I been tryin' to reach you all weekend, but you don't answer. You duck me last night. I want to know what your problem is." They passed the newsstand, the liquor store, and Mio's before Marnyke said anything.

"I was out of town," Marnyke told her.

"Where you go? Disneyland?" Sherise responded. "You coulda answered your cell phone."

"I didn't want anyone to know." Marnyke's heels clicked against the uneven sidewalk. They came to the corner of Satchel Paige Drive and had to wait for the light to change.

"That don't make no sense," Sherise shot back.

The light changed; they crossed the busy street.

"It makes sense if you was me," Marnyke mumbled.

"Why don't you speak English, Marnyke, instead of nonsense?"

"Okay, fine," Marnyke said defiantly. "You really gotta get in my business? My sis and I took the bus to Sandersville to visit my mom. You happy now?"

Sherise's jaw dropped open. Sandersville was where the big state prisons were.

That's right. Marnyke's mom was doing time. Busted for selling crack, selling her body for crack, or selling both, Sherise didn't remember.

Every Friday night, buses left from the city depot to go to Sandersville. People would ride up and spend the whole weekend. There were all these cheap motels that made money from families visiting inmates. Sherise had never been, but she'd sure heard about it.

"Don't believe me? Ask my sis," Marnyke insisted as they continued along Twenty-Third Street. Marnyke kept her voice down so the other kids wouldn't hear. "That's why I wasn't at Mio's, and that's why no one could reach me. I ain't got nothin' to do wit' no boy chasing you. You think I've never had a guy set on me, Sherise? Followin' me home? Beggin' my digits? Sendin' flowers I don't want? Not leavin' me alone even if I say so? Think, Sherise! I'd never do that to another girl!"

Well. That made sense. Kinda.

But what about how Marnyke had laughed in the cafetorium? What was that? Was it because she helped ruin the yearbook in the first place?

Sherise asked her.

Marnyke banged her own head with her fist. "Okay, you're right. I messed that up. Truth is, you and your sis, you have like the perfect life. You have perfect parents. You got the perfect boyfriend. What do I got? I got guys who want a piece of me but don't even want to hear me say 'boo!', a sister who's about to get married, and a mom in the big house. I was glad you was catchin' some hell, Sherise. I'm not proud of that, but I was glad."

They walked little more. Sherise looked back at Kiki who made a "what's goin' on?" gesture with her hands. Sherise waved her off. She'd tell her later.

Finally, they got to school.

"I'm sorry," Marnyke said. "I shouldn't have laughed at you."

Sherise found herself telling Marnyke that it was okay.

In a way it was okay.

With all her problems? With the stalker? With the yearbook? With losing her job? She wouldn't trade her life with Marnyke for anything.

CHAPTER 10

The school day passed in a blur. At every moment Sherise had friends at her side. At lunch she was surrounded. Her cell phone stayed quiet. She felt safe. Mostly.

But as the minutes ticked away and four thirty got closer, the little knot in her stomach turned into a bird's nest of worry. By the time the final bell sounded, her feet were cold and her hands shaky.

She couldn't go right to Northeast Towers, though. There was a YC meeting first. Ms. O had said that Mr. Crandall wanted to say a few words to everyone.

Sherise would have to say something too.

Gee. Fun.

The meeting was in Ms. O's room. Everyone was there. Mr. Crandall was waiting for them when they arrived. He rapped his hairy hand on the desk as he spoke.

"I talked to the printer," he said. "Evidently, there was some sort of hacking that caused the yearbook to be printed with that, um, picture in it. If it turns out that any of you people had anything to do with it, I'll have you expelled, and there'll never be another yearbook printed again. Don't try me!"

The guidance counselor stomped away.

The room was still. Sherise, who sat in the front row by Nishell, turned around to look at Marnyke. Today Marnyke wasn't laughing.

Ms. O talked next. "That was super fun!" she commented wryly.

Everyone laughed uneasily.

"I can say that because I am so confident that not a single South Central student was involved," Ms. O declared.

Tia raised her hand. "Yeah. But unless it gets figured out, Crandall's gonna blame us."

Ms. O nodded. "Possibly. But as we say in Nigeria, 'One must paddle in the boat that one has.'"

"Will we still be considered for the big award?" Kiki called out.

"I don't see any reason why not," Ms. O told them.

There was actual applause after that. Then the classroom door opened. Sherise swallowed hard, thinking that Mr. Crandall was coming back for another round. But it wasn't Mr. Crandall. It was Carlos. He'd never come to a YC meeting before.

She gave him a little wave. He nodded and slid into a seat in the back.

Sherise raised her hand. Ms. O called on her. Sherise stood and faced the other members of the YC. Something that Crandall had said—that if it was up to him, there wouldn't be another yearbook printed ever—had given her a great idea. Whoever had messed up the yearbook should not be allowed to win.

"I just gotta say," Sherise told them, "I'm so grateful to all of you for standin' by me and standin' by each other. It would have been easy to come apart over this, but YC stuck together."

"That's nice and all, Sherise, but it ain't gonna get everyone a yearbook!" Jackson called.

Sherise managed a smile. "I've got an idea about that. I think we build a website. We put the whole yearbook up so anyone with a computer or a smart phone can look at it. With all the good pages—"

"Crandall'll have a fit," Tia interrupted.

"He's having a fit anyway," Sherise pointed out. "Look. The seniors already got their yearbooks. After they graduate, there's nothing Crandall can do to stop one of them from building a website with the yearbook on it." She marched over and stood by Darnell who was graduating in a few weeks. "Right, Darnell?"

Darnell shook his head helplessly. "I don't got no 'puter skills."

"You a smart boy who's goin' to college on a scholarship. You find someone who do to help you. Good idea, everyone?"

It was better than a good idea. It was a great idea. The whole YC club whooped and hollered. Sherise saw her sister and Carlos look at her with admiration.

You paddle in the boat you got. This be our boat.

She checked the time. Four o'clock. Just enough time for her to be walked home and to get into place under the tree by the basketball court.

Just enough time to be bait.

As she took her seat again, she pushed away a bead of nervous sweat on her forehead. There was another boat. And she'd be the only one in it.

"Fine," Sherise thought. "Gimme the damn paddle."

The bait was in place. The trap was set.

As Sherise walked over to the bench under the big tree, she saw her friends stationed all over the courtyard. Meanwhile, on the court itself, Tyson was playing ball with some men from the community association. Then, as she sat, she noticed a police cruiser stop on the street with a clear sightline to her bench.

Wow. Tyson and my mom must have gone back to the cops. This time they listened!

She was surrounded. Maybe too surrounded. The stalker had to realize that she was being watched.

Would he even show?

"How you doing down there?" a male voice called to her softly.

Sherise looked up. Carlos was eight feet above her in the tree, nearly hidden in a tangle of branches and leaves. He'd insisted on being there.

"He makes one bad move, Sherise," Carlos had reminded, "I'm comin' down right on his head."

She gave him an OK sign. Suddenly, she saw Carlos scramble a little higher in the tree. What the—

"Hi, Sherise."

She turned.

A short, skinny dude was standing in front of her. He had short hair and glasses. He wore nice pants and the kind of white shirt that guys wore to church. He seemed about her age. There was something familiar about him she couldn't place. Not till he spoke again.

"I've been wanting to send you flowers since we were in Mrs. Duke's class," he said. "I finally got the courage."

Omigod. Mrs. Duke's class? That was third grade at Hesby Elementary!

Now she knew who her stalker was. It was Conrad Shipkins, the nerdy kid who'd had a super crush on her in grade school and then had moved to Detroit to become some kind of computer super brainiac. Last Friday she'd gotten a nice note from him on BlackPlanet.

Conrad is my stalker? You gotta be kidding!

She saw Tyson and the guys on the basketball court move toward her, but she gently waved them off. Conrad wasn't dangerous. A little strange, maybe, since he was so smart. But not dangerous.

___

"Why don't you sit, Conrad? You know you been scaring the crap outta me," Sherise told him, motioning to the bench.

Conrad sat. "I didn't know how else to get your attention."

"Well, you got it all right," Sherise admitted with a little laugh. "How'd you pick this weekend to show up? 'Cause my life's kinda nuts right now. You must know what's going on with the yearbook. Everybody knows."

Conrad looked nervous. "Well, um, er ..."

"Come on, Conrad," Sherise urged. "You owe me after what you've been doing."

"Well, er ... that thing with the year-book? That's kinda my fault too."

Say what?

"Conrad, whatchu sayin'?"

"I'd better explain," Conrad sighed.

Sherise nodded. "That would be a good idea."

He turned to face her. The afternoon sun glinted off his glasses. "Well, it probably wasn't such a good thing, looking back and all, but I've never forgotten you. I've always liked you. I always try to keep up on what's going on with you."

"Go on," Sherise urged.

"So when I heard about your yearbook being in that contest, and I knew that you were the head of the yearbook club, I thought maybe I could do something that would get your attention. I could get everyone mad at you. Then I'd show up, and I wouldn't be mad at you. I'd just be your biggest fan, and then you'd want to be with me. Except it didn't work." Conrad looked ashamed.

Sherise put two-and-two together. "Oh no, Conrad. Tell me you weren't the one who—"

"Big Boss needs a better password on his server than one-two-three-four-five," Conrad observed drily.

She couldn't believe it was Conrad. Conrad!

He kept talking. "Once I was into the server, it was easy to Photoshop a picture of Crandall, upload it, and make the change. I hear everyone hates him anyway."

"You hear right."

"I guess I'm going to be in trouble now," Conrad confessed. "I saw a lot of people I used to know on the way over here. They're watching right now. But I just had to talk to you."

Sherise tried to figure out what to do. Quickly, she made a decision.

"Conrad, I could have you arrested," she told him. "There's a whole lotta people 'round here now who want that. I kinda want that. Crandall will definitely want that. But I'll tell you what," she offered, knowing Carlos was in the tree overhead and could hear every word. "You go home to Michigan, leave me alone, and use your computer genius brain to let Crandall know that he got punk'd long-range. I'll let this go."

"I can do that!" Conrad said eagerly.

"I thought you could," Sherise agreed. "And next time? Find a girl to impress who don't have a boyfriend. Okay?"

"Okay," he said.

"Hey! One more thing!" she added quickly.

"What's that?"

Sherise thought about her idea of putting the yearbook up online.

"If a friend of mine needed help settin' up a website, could you do it for him?"

Conrad nodded. "In my sleep."

Sherise put out her hand for a shake. Conrad took it. They shook on what had to be the strangest deal of Sherise's life.

Even though there was school the next day, that night there was a rooftop party at Northeast Towers to celebrate the solving of the mysteries. The whole YC was there. In fact, it seemed to Sherise like the whole school came. Everyone brought food and drinks. Jackson ran the music. Darnell did his thing on the mic. As the sun went down, the roof was a mass of kids getting down to a hot dance mix.

Tyson and LaTreece chaperoned, along with some of the men who'd watched out for Sherise that afternoon. Another time Sherise might have been annoyed at all the adults. Tonight, considering some of her classmates who were on the roof and how much they liked to get down with herb and Jose C, maybe it was a good thing.

After nightfall Jackson put on Marvin Gaye's "Sexual Healing." Carlos took Sherise by the arm and led her onto the part of the roof where kids were dancing. She saw Tia in close with Ty Kessler. Nishell got Jackson out from behind the deejay area to dance with her. Even Kiki was dancing with this boy she liked who'd moved across town, Cyril Davis.

She swayed in Carlos's strong arms and gazed up at him. "I liked you in the tree today."

"I liked being there," he agreed. "But there's one thing I gotta know."

"Just ask."

Carlos grinned. "You ever kiss that boy?"

"Carlos!" She swatted his butt. "It was grade school. He used to pull my hair to show me he liked me."

———

"I bet no one ever kissed you like this. Ever."

He leaned down and touched his lips to hers. It felt electric and so hot her knees weakened.

"Um, no," she said when the kiss was over. "No one ever kissed me that way."

He moved toward her again. She got ready for a repeat and prayed she wouldn't faint from how he made her feel.

"Good," he whispered.

He brought his lips to hers once more. Just as they touched, her cell rang.

Who could be calling? Everyone she knew was there.

She edged away from Carlos and took her phone out of the black pants she'd changed into for the party. She looked at caller ID.

Unavailable.

Oh no. It has to be Conrad, back for another round.

She thrust the phone at Carlos. "You answer. I think it's Conrad again. I can't deal now. I really can't!"

Carlos took the phone and narrowed his eyes, ready to ream Conrad Shipkins a new one. "Hello?"

Sherise watched as Carlos's face went from anger to surprise to pleasure as he listened. Then, without saying a word, he clicked off.

"So?" she demanded. "Was it him?"

"Come with me," he said.

"Where to? Don't tell me that Conrad's here!"

"Just come."

He took one of her hands and walked them out of the crowd as the Marvin Gaye song ended and Jackson spun into some Pac Div. The bass pounded so hard the rooftop shook. Carlos led her around to the far side of the elevator shaft.

There was someone waiting for her there.

Not Conrad.

Juanita!

"Hey, Sherise," Juanita said. She was wearing one of her tight orange skirts and a black tank top with no bra. She looked as hot as any of the high school girls. No gloves either. Her tats were totally visible.

"Hey, yourself." Sherise couldn't believe her old boss had come.

"I heard you had a rough weekend," Juanita said.

"A little."

"I got your e-mail. Thanks for that," Juanita told her. "That was the right thing to do."

Sherise nodded. "You're welcome."

Juanita rearranged her hair behind one ear. "You did the right thing. I want to do the right thing. If you want to come back, I could really use you." She looked at Carlos. "And you too. On a trial basis, that is. Don't mess up 'cause it'll mess me up bad. You know what I'm saying?"

Carlos nodded as Sherise thanked Juanita.

"Is that a yes?" Juanita asked.

"Yes for me," Sherise said. She looked at Carlos. "I'd love it if you said yes too. But it's up to you."

"What do you say, Carlos?" Juanita asked.

Carlos smiled. "Let me check with my probation officer and call you tomorrow. If she says cool, I'm good."

Juanita nodded. "My pleasure. See you at work tomorrow, Sherise."

They watched her leave. When she was gone, Sherise punched the air. "Yes! I got my job back! No daycare duty!"

The music was still pounding. "Wanna dance?" Carlos asked.

Sherise shook her head. "Let's stay here for a minute."

She turned and leaned against the fence that surrounded the rooftop many stories above the city. They were looking west. Sherise saw a familiar bright object in the sky close to the horizon.

"Look, Starman. There's Venus." She pointed.

As she pointed, a white light streaked across the sky above the bright planet, leaving a gorgeous glowing tail that lingered before it disappeared.

Wow! Was that a—

"Congrats," Carlos told her. "You just saw a shooting star. Meteor, actually. A piece of a rock from outer space that burns up in our atmosphere. That what makes the tail."

Quickly, Sherise closed her eyes and thought of something she really wanted.

"Did you just make a wish on a shooting star?" Carlos mock-accused when she'd opened her eyes again.

Sherise nodded shyly.

"For what?" he asked, his voice coy.

"For this." She turned her lips up to his and closed her eyes.

Her wish came true. Again. And again. And again.